THE MANY LIVES OF
CHIO AND GORO

THE MANY LIVES OF

CHIO AND GORO

BETTY JEAN LIFTON

Illustrated by **YASUO SEGAWA**

W · W · NORTON & COMPANY · INC · NEW YORK

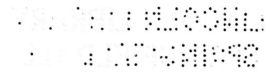

Books by Betty Jean Lifton

Joji and the Amanojaku

The Rice-Cake Rabbit

The Many Lives of Chio and Goro

For Karen —

in her new life.

Once upon a time,
in a village in Japan,
there lived an old farmer
named Goro,
and his wife,
Chio.

They had no children.
In fact,
they had no one in all the world,
except each other.

Chio was a very good wife.

    During the day

        she worked in the fields with Goro,

    and every night

        she cooked rice for his dinner.

But Chio had a very bad memory,

    and she was always crying to Goro:

        "Hie ho da dum dum, hie ho da dee,

        I've forgot something; what could it be?"

One night

while Chio and Goro lay on their mats

on the floor,

they talked about what they would be

in their next life,

for they knew that their time in this world

was almost spent.

"In my next life,"

said Goro,

"I will be a fox,

for the fox is a shrewd animal

and gets his food faster

than the farmer who bends

over the fields all day."

"Then I will also be a fox

in my next life,"

said Chio.

"And I will be clever as a fox

and never forget anything."

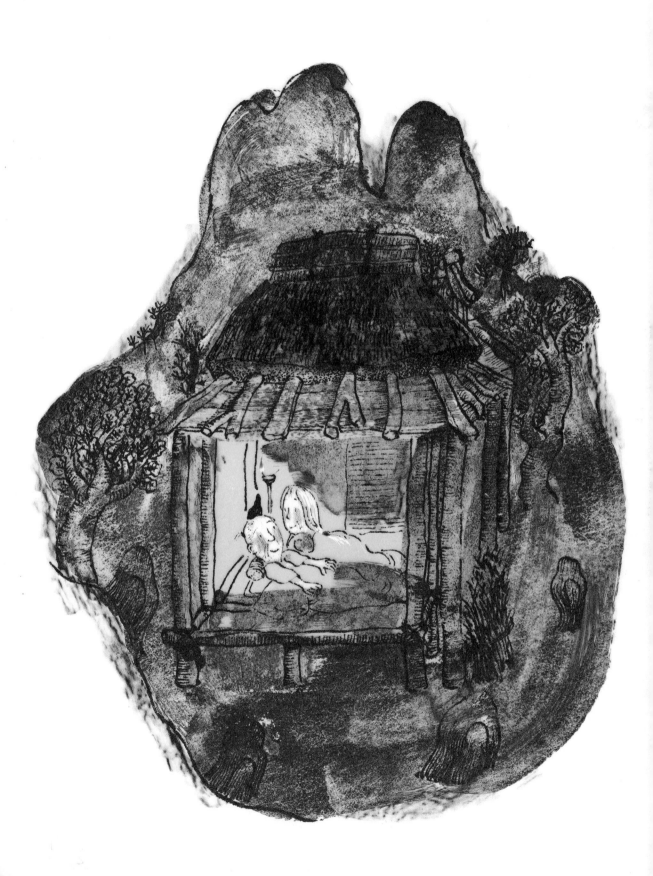

After they had decided to be foxes,

Chio and Goro went to sleep.

And a few hours later,

when all the stars were dancing merrily

over the farmhouse,

Goro slipped away

into his next life.

And that same night,
in a nearby forest,
a tiny red fox
was born to a mother fox.

Chio was very lonely without Goro
and made plans to join him
as soon as possible.

She sold the house,
and sorted her things,
and said her good-byes,
but just when she was ready to go,
she suddenly remembered
that she could not remember
what animal they had decided to be.

Poor Chio!

She paced up and down, back and forth,

crying:

"Hie ho da dum dum, hie ho da dee,

I've forgot what animal to be!"

She named all the animals she could think of —

the dog?

the cat?

the dragon?

the rabbit?

the bear?

the bull?

the horse?

But it was no use.

She could not remember!

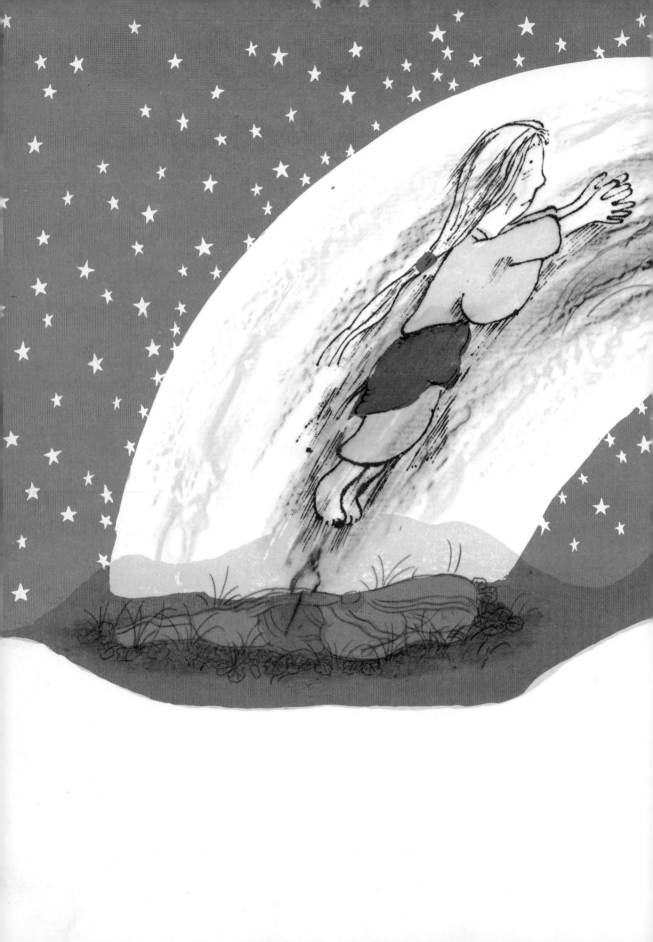

Finally,

    she was so tired,

        she gave up trying,

            and with her last breath

                she decided

                    that in her next life

                        she would be

                            a CHICKEN!

And that same night,
in a nearby farmyard,
a tiny golden chick
was born to a mother hen.

Meanwhile,

Goro, the little fox,

grew bigger and stronger every day,

until

he was old enough to hunt his own food.

Then his mother took him out
and taught him how
   to jump a fence,
   and sniff the ground,
   and smell the wind,
   and follow the path
   that led to the chicken coop
   in the nearby farmyard.

One dark spring night
    Goro's mother said,
        "Son, it's time for you
            to prove yourself a fox.
        Go down to the nearby farmyard,
            and snatch a plump young chicken."

Goro's heart thumped wildly with excitement.
    He stole stealthily through the trees,
        his nose to the ground,
        his ears perked high,
        his tail slung out,
        just as his mother had taught him.

Just beyond

Goro could see

the proud mother hen

parading in front

of the hen house

with all her dear

little chicks.

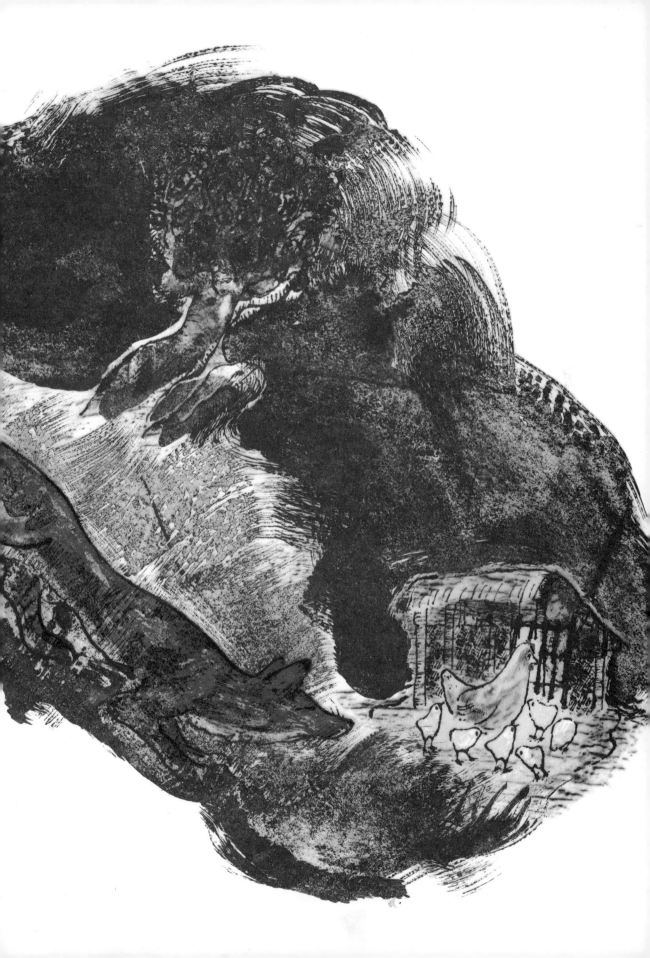

Goro moved closer and closer.

But his foot touched some twigs,

Crunch! Crunch! Crunch!

and the mother hen shouted,

"Fox! Fox! Fox!"

and all the chicks ran helter-skelter

into the hen house.

That is, all except one,

named Chio.

This chicken had such a bad memory
that even now,
in this moment of danger,
she couldn't remember how to find
the door of the hen house.
She circled round and round and round
in great confusion and fright.

Goro quickly jumped over the fence
  into the chicken coop,
    and crouched low ready to spring
      on this foolish chicken,
  when suddenly she began to cry:
    "Hie ho da dum dum, hie ho da dee,
    I've forgot where the hen door could be!"

A cold chill ran through Goro's body!

His fur stood on end!

And then with a shrill yowl,

he jumped out of the farmyard

into the forest,

and ran breathlessly

all the way home.

Goro's mother was furious
      when he returned to their den
            without a chicken.
She growled at him angrily,
      and sent him to bed
            without any supper.

Poor Goro,

he was a failure.

He had been outfoxed by a silly chicken.

All his fox friends sneered when he passed by.

No one would talk to him.

No one would play with him.

No one would hunt with him.

Goro became so miserable,

he could not eat or sleep.

Soon he was just a shadow of his former self.

But sometimes during the day,
  Goro would find himself
    hiding behind a tree
      to watch Chio, that giddy chicken,
    running around in circles, crying:
      "Hie ho da dum dum, hie ho da dee,
      I've forgot where the hen door could be!"

The more he heard Chio's song,
  the more Goro liked her,
    and the more he liked her,
      the more miserable he felt,
    for a chicken-hearted fox
      is no good to anyone —
        least of all, to himself.

Finally,
when he was nothing but fur and bones,
Goro knew that his days in this world
were already numbered.
That night
he decided that in his next life
he would be a rooster!

And a few hours later,
when all the stars were dancing merrily
over the fox's den,
Goro slipped away
into his next life.

And that same night,
in a nearby farmyard,
a tiny red rooster
was born to a mother hen.

It was, of course, Goro.

He grew into a handsome red rooster

with a comb so high and a tail so long,

that all the hens fluttered

when he strutted by.

But Goro had eyes for only one hen —
> Chio.

And one day when he heard her crying:
>> "Hie ho da dum dum, hie ho da dee,
>> I've forgot where the hen door could be!"

he gallantly strutted up, bowed low,
and escorted her right to the door.

Chio was so flustered
   that she consented to be his wife.
   And before very long they had
      dozens of baby chickens
running over the barnyard.

Chio was a very good mother,

    but every few days she would cry:

        "Hie ho da dum dum, hie ho da dee,

        I've forgot where my babies could be!"

And then Goro would go to the hen-house door

    and show her they were all inside.

One day,

    when they were getting old,

        Goro said to Chio:

            "In my next life I will be a man,

                for a man is more talented than a rooster,

                    and has much more to crow about."

            "Then I will be a woman

              in my next life,"

                said Chio,

            "and I promise to become your wife

            and never to forget anything."

And a few hours later,
when all the stars were dancing merrily
over the farmyard,
they both slipped away
into the next life.

And that same night,
in a nearby village,
a baby boy named Goro
was born to a wealthy lord.

And at the same time
a baby girl named Chio
was born to that lord's friend.

When Chio and Goro were still children,
their parents brought them to the festival
at their village shrine.

But Chio became lost in the crowd,

and Goro found her crying:

"Hie ho da dum dum, hie ho da dee,

I've forgot where the shrine gate could be."

Goro led her right up to the gate,

and she bowed shyly.

And when they grew up,

they were married,

and lived happily ever after —

until the next life.